Santalicious

by Stig Kristensen
and Tracy Hare

make believe ideas

All wrapped up

Doodle bows and patterns on the presents.

Filled with fun!

Fill these stockings with gifts.

Stylish snowman!

Doodle a hat and gloves for the snowman.

Ooh La La!

Gorgeous garlands

Decorate the tree with doodles.

Perfect presents!

what's under the tree?

Merry Christmas

cool

PRESENT

from

GIFT

Amazing antlers

Doodle antlers on the reindeer!

Seasons greetings

Design two beautiful christmas cards.

White Christmas?

Doodle snowflakes on the windowpane.

Frosty feet!

Doodle more footprints in the snow.

Winter warmers!

Cute

happy holidays

Doodle patterns on the cozy mittens.

All I want for Christmas!

Draw your dream gift in the parcel.

Winter warmer!

Doodle flames on the open fire.

Soft 'n' snug!

Design a special holiday sweater!

cool

Cute

dress up

Winter

Noel

Special delivery!

Fill Santa's sleigh with parcels.

The 1st day of Christmas

Doodle leaves and pears in the tree.

Shining star

Doodle a star
on top of the tree.

Tasty treats

Fill the bowls with fancy snacks.

delicious!

mmmm!

yummy...

Christmas kiss!

who's under the mistletoe?

Happy New Year!

Doodle fireworks in the sky
to celebrate the New Year!

WOW

Super sleigh

Doodle decorations on Santa's sleigh.

Christmas chimes

Doodle some pretty patterns on the bells.

Come on in!

Design a holiday wreath for the door.

Winter wonderland

what is growing in the garden?

NORTH POLE

The 2nd day of Christmas

surround the two turtle doves with hearts and flowers.

Totally crackers

Decorate the crackers.

Ooh La La!

Christmas candy

delicious!

Doodle designs on the candy canes.

mmmm!

i like sweet things

yummy...

Super snowmen!

Doodle heads and hats on the snowmen.

Festive faces!

dress up

cool

I ♥ SANTA

Cute

Doodle faces for these Christmas characters.

Stylish Santa

Decorate Santa's coat with beautiful doodles.

To you from me . . .

GIFT

what's inside the parcels?

Cute

from

Star of wonder!

Doodle designs inside the star.

Festive frame

Decorate the holiday window.

Tasty treats

delicious!

Doodle candy in the jar.

yummy...

I like sweet
things

mmmm!

Crunch time!

Doodle some carrots for the reindeers.

delicious!

yummy...

mmmm!

This Way!

Doodle a sign for Santa.

The 5th day of Christmas

Doodle gems on the five gold rings

Special stockings

cool

Cute

Doodle special socks for christmas Day.

Happy holly-day

cake

Doodle more holly and berries on the christmas cakes.

yummy...

Deck the door . . .

happy holidays

Decorate the door for christmas.

Noel

Jingle Bells

Let it snow!

Doodle a wintry scene in the snow globe.

Cute

NORTH POLE

That's entertainment!

what does Santa watch on TV?

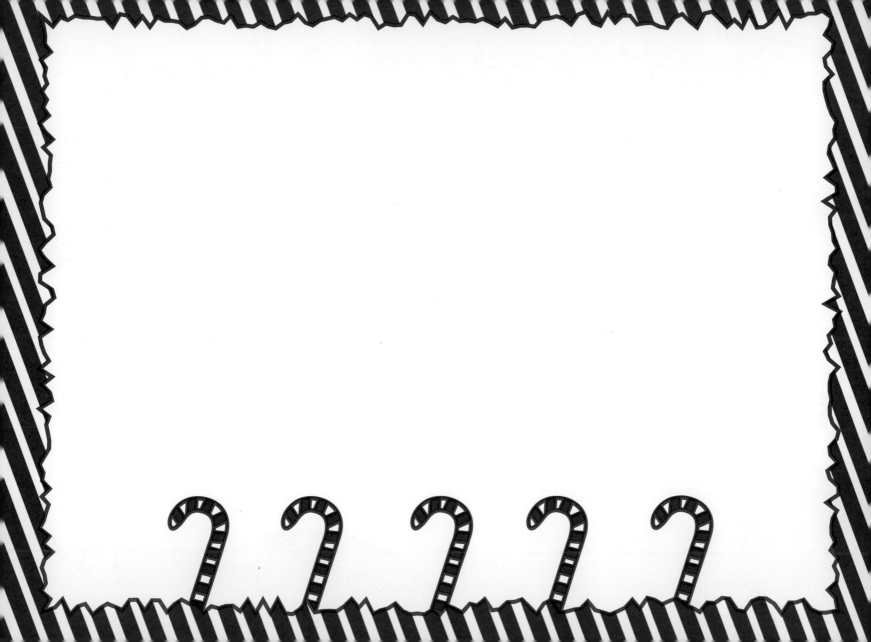

Crazy candles

Decorate the candles like candy canes!

Shine a light!

Doodle fancy-shaped lights.

Christmas china

Doodle a special holiday design for the cup and saucer.

Post it!

Design some special christmas stamps.

Piles of presents!

Add more gifts to the stack.

The 7th day of Christmas

Doodle feathers on the swans.

Pretty please!

write a letter to Santa and decorate it with doodles.

for you!

PRESENT

from

Merry Christmas

HoHoHo!

Doodle christmas patterns in the letters.

Fancy frosting

mmmm!

Decorate the christmas cupcakes.

yummy...

cake

Christmas cookies!

Doodle frosting and sprinkles on the cookies.

Sweet treat!

mmmm!

delicious!

Doodle chocolates in the box.

yummy...

Over the top?

create a light display on the roof!

Window dressing

All wrapped up!

Doodle coats to keep the reindeer warm.

Cute

Noel

Jingle Bells

Dear Santa . . .

GIFT

Doodle your christmas wish!

from

PRESENT

Holiday hats

Doodle patterns for Santa's hats.

cool

happy
holidays

Fabulous flowers

Merry Christmas

Pretty +rx

Beautiful

♡

Noel

Fill the vase with a festive display!

Wonder wings

Doodle the fairies some wings.

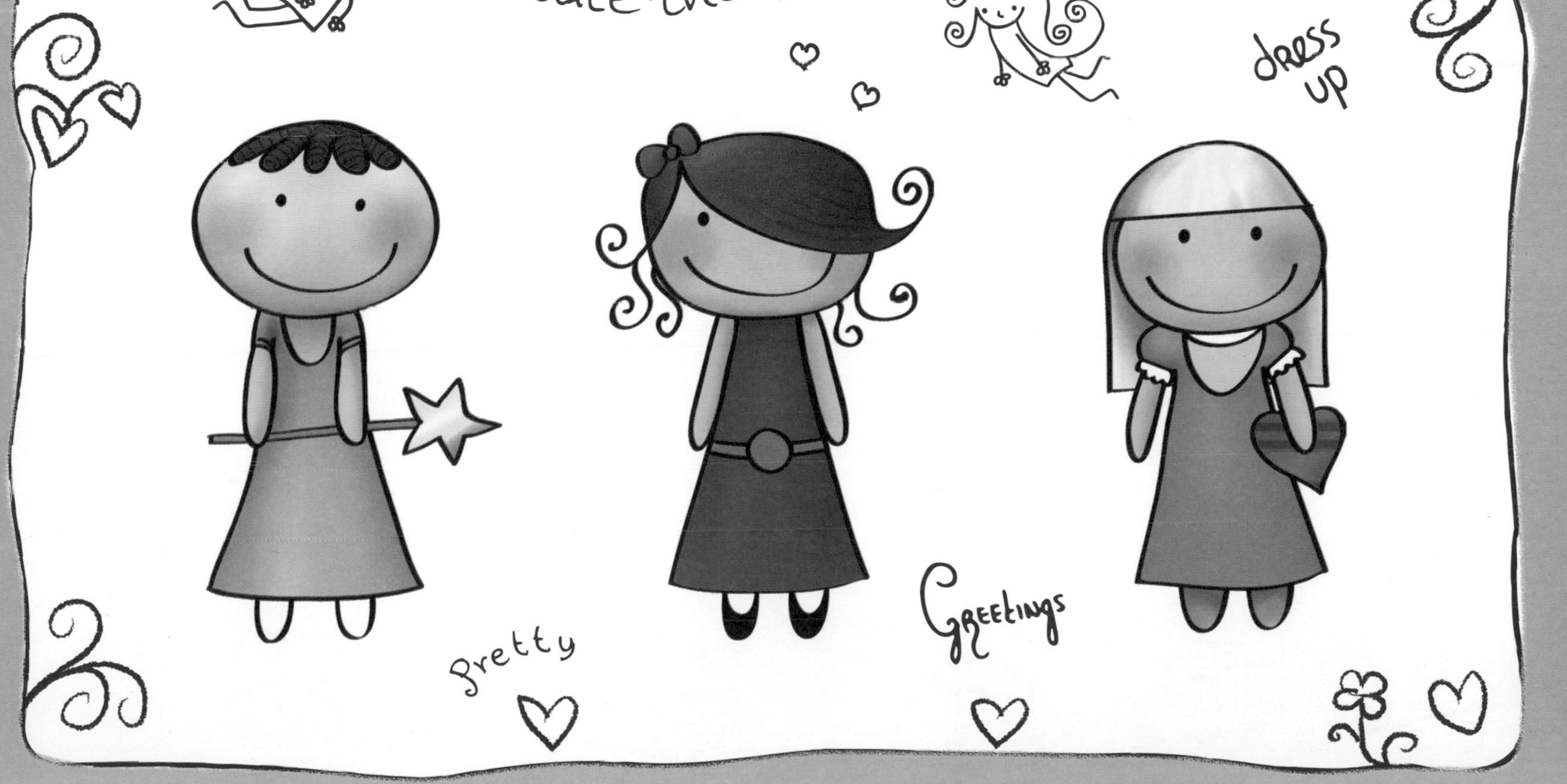

Fabulous feet!

Doodle some new boots for Santa.

I ♥ SANTA

Cute

Ooh La La!

Nice ice

Doodle more icicles hanging from the trees!

Delightful decorations

Doodle patterns and draw more ornaments.

Perfect pines

Doodle more pine cones in the bowl.

Gorgeous glow

Doodle more lovely lanterns.

Peace on Earth

Fill the page with angels.

Terrific tree!

Decorate the tree with doodle garlands.

Holiday hideaway
Doodle a door and windows on the cozy cottage.